The Fairy House

Fairy Sleepover

Welcome to the Fairy House –
a whole new magical world...

Have you got all *The Fairy House* books?

☐ FAIRY FRIENDS
☐ FAIRY FOR A DAY
☐ FAIRIES TO THE RESCUE
☐ FAIRY RIDING SCHOOL
☐ FAIRY SLEEPOVER
☐ FAIRY JEWELS
☐ FAIRY PARTY
☐ FAIRY FLYING LESSONS

Make sure you visit www.thefairyhouse.co.uk
for competitions, prizes and lots more fairy fun!

The Fairy House

Fairy Sleepover

Kelly McKain

Illustrated by Nicola Slater

SCHOLASTIC

First published in the UK in 2008 by Scholastic Children's Books
An imprint of Scholastic Ltd
Euston House, 24 Eversholt Street
London, NW1 1DB, UK
Registered office: Westfield Road, Southam, Warwickshire, CV47 0RA
SCHOLASTIC and associated logos are trademarks and or registered trademarks of
Scholastic Inc.
This edition published in 2009

ISBN 978 1 407 10890 2

A CIP catalogue record for this book is available from the British Library

Printed in the UK by CPI Bookmarque, Croydon, CR0 4TD
Papers used by Scholastic Children's Books are made from wood grown in
sustainable forests.

1 3 5 7 9 10 8 6 4 2

www.kellymckain.co.uk
www.scholastic.co.uk/zone

For

Perdi and Felicity, with love xx

Chapter 1

When Katie got back from the shops with Mum on Saturday morning she helped put everything away as quickly as she could, then hurried outside. A tangle of bindweed now covered the wire fence that separated her back garden from the almost-meadow beyond. She was filled with excitement as she wriggled under the wire and swished through the high grass and bright flowers.

The almost-meadow was the only

1

patch of wild land that hadn't been built on in the whole of the new estate. No one ever went there and since she and Mum had moved into their little house a couple of months before, it had become Katie's private place. Summer was now in full swing and the blue sky was alive with singing birds, buzzing bees and beautiful butterflies. And there, under the green canopy of the old oak tree, stood the most beautiful, colourful, *magical* thing of all – the Fairy House.

When Katie had accidentally left her dolls' house under the oak tree one night, she'd never dreamt that *fairies* would move in.

She hadn't even thought they existed – not in real life, anyway. But here they were, four of them, called Snowdrop, Bluebell, Rosehip and Daisy. She still found it hard to believe that they were really living in the almost-meadow at the bottom of her garden!

When she spotted her four friends under the old oak tree, she couldn't help wondering what they were up to. They had pulled the bathtub out of the house and were all standing inside it, knee deep in

bright pink . . . well, bright pink *something*. And they were treading up and down vigorously.

"Hi! Erm, what on earth are you doing?" she asked them.

"Making wild strawberry juice!" cried Rosehip, the flame-haired autumn fairy.

"And we could use an extra pair of feet!" added Bluebell, stomping hard.

Grinning, Katie carefully crouched down beside the Fairy House and put her little finger on the tiny blue door handle, which Snowdrop, the winter fairy, had bewitched with fairy dust.

"I believe in fairies, I believe in fairies, I believe in fairies," she chanted. With these magic words there was a tingle at the top of her head and a whooshing in her ears.

In seconds she had shrunk down, down, down to *fairy size!*

"Come on, jump in!" cried Daisy, the gentle summer fairy. "It's fun!"

So Katie kicked off her shoes and rolled her jeans up and climbed into the bath of pink juice. She put her arms round Snowdrop and Bluebell (who, with her bright blue hair and sparkly eyes, was the bravest of the fairies – and the naughtiest by far!) and copied her friends' stamping. The wild strawberries squelched

between her toes and a sweet, ripe, *pink* smell wafted into the air.

"This *is* fun!" she giggled. "But what's it for?"

"Wild strawberry juice is used for lots of things," Snowdrop explained. "You can dye fabrics with it, or wear it as perfume, or even drink it."

"Ew, yuck!" Katie cried. "I wouldn't fancy that – not after our feet have been in it!"

The fairies all laughed.

"Fairy feet are very clean, as a matter of fact," said Rosehip. "Well, except Bluebell's, which *are* smelly!"

"They are not!" cried Bluebell indignantly. "*Yours* are, you mean!"

"Are not!" Rosehip retaliated.

It looked like one of their famous arguments was brewing, so Katie quickly changed the subject. "Do you remember a girl called Lily

Rose?" she asked, still treading the strawberry pulp.

"Oh, yes, she's lovely," Daisy replied, and the others agreed.

Just the week before, Rosehip had trained Katie to horse-ride by using fairy dust to bring her toy ponies to life. She'd entered a gymkhana on a real pony called Ebony, and met Lily Rose afterwards. They'd quickly become firm friends, and Ebony had become Lily Rose's very own pony.

"Well, she's coming over tonight and we're having a sleepover – isn't that great?" said Katie.

"Yeah! Great!" cried the fairies enthusiastically.

Katie smiled. "You don't know what a sleepover *is*, do you?" she asked them, and they had to admit that they didn't.

"Well, it's when you have a friend to stay for the whole night and you

play games and have a midnight feast and tell secrets," Katie explained. "We're having ours in a tent in the garden!"

The fairies got truly excited then.

"Brilliant!" cried Daisy. "I'll bring my glowing daisy lights in case it's a bit scary in the dark."

"And Rosehip and I can bring our bedspreads for us all to sleep under," added Bluebell.

Katie's heart sank. She felt terrible. Of course she should have realized that the fairies would want to come to the sleepover. And of course they couldn't. She stopped stamping the strawberies and sat down heavily on the side of the bath.

"And I know this fabulous game where you—" Snowdrop was saying, but Katie interrupted her.

"It's not that I don't *want* you to come," she began, "it's just that, well. . ." She stared down at the strawberry slosh between her toes, feeling four pairs of eyes on her. "You *know* no one can find out about you," she muttered.

"But Lily Rose won't tell. . ." Rosehip began.

"No one can know. Not even Lily Rose," Katie insisted, giving them a stern look. "It might jeopardize the fairy task."

But the fairies looked far from convinced.

"It doesn't say anything on our scroll from the Fairy Queen about not telling anyone," said Snowdrop.

She pulled a roll of paper out of the secret pocket hidden among the petals of her silky skirt and unfurled it.

Fairy Task No. 45826

By Royal Command of the Fairy Queen

Terrible news has reached Fairyland. As
you know, the Magic Oak is the gateway
between Fairyland and the human world. The
sparkling whirlwind can only drop fairies off
here. Humans plan to knock down our special
tree and build a house on the land. If this
happens, fairies will no longer be able to
come and help people and the environment.
You must stop them from doing this terrible
thing and make sure that the tree is
protected for the future. Only then will you
be allowed back into Fairyland.

By order of Her Eternal Majesty
The Fairy Queen

PS You will need one each of the twelve
birthstones to work the magic that will save
the tree - but hurry, there's not much time!

She read it aloud and then folded her arms and said, "See?"

Katie sighed. "I'm sorry, but we can't take the risk. We're doing so well – we've got four birthstones already, and we've found out that the revolting Tiffany's father, Max Towner, is the one who wants to knock down the tree. Just think about it – what if Lily Rose accidentally let it slip, to just one person, that you exist?"

"So? That wouldn't matter!" said Rosehip defiantly.

"But imagine if that person told another person, who told another person, who told Tiffany Towner, who told Max? And what if Max Towner captured you, to stop you from saving the Magic Oak tree? Then you couldn't complete the

fairy task and save Fairyland. And you know what that would mean. . ."

The fairies' eyes widened. If fairies couldn't come to earth any more to look after the weather and the plants and the soil, there would be hurricanes and floods and nothing would grow. It would be a disaster for everyone on earth. They couldn't even *think* about not completing the fairy task.

The four of them were silent after that. They didn't want to admit it, but they knew Katie was right – they really *couldn't* come to the sleepover.

Suddenly Bluebell stamped her foot angrily, splattering wild strawberry juice all over everyone. "I don't care anyway," she shouted. "Sleepy-overs sound stupid and boring, so there!"

Daisy, Rosehip and Snowdrop

looked ever so glum.

Katie nudged Rosehip, trying to make her smile, and said, "Oh, come on, cheer up. I've still got an hour before Lily Rose arrives. We could start working out how to get another birthstone."

"I don't feel like it," she said huffily. "I'm going to play the piano instead."

She fluttered out of the bath, strawberry feet dripping, and zoomed into the Fairy House. Katie winced as the sound of angry twanging filled the air.

Not to be outdone by Rosehip, Bluebell flew straight up to a branch of the old oak tree and hung upside down, sulking.

Katie turned to friendly, kind Daisy, but even *she* had stomped off across the grass and wrapped

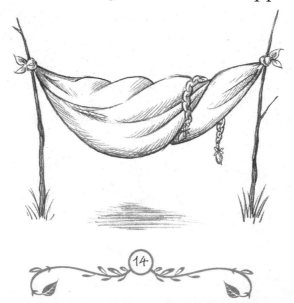

herself up in her hammock.

"Snowdrop, surely *you* aren't upset," Katie cried, exasperated.

She tugged at Snowdrop's silky skirt, but the little fairy busied herself with pouring the wild strawberry juice into small glass bottles, pretending not to hear her.

Katie suddenly felt really cross. She'd had enough of being sulked at and ignored. "Fine! Be like that, then! See if I care!"

She stormed over to the Fairy House, grabbed the door handle and muttered the magic words. As soon as she'd turned big again, she stomped off home, all trace of her happy mood gone.

Chapter 2

When Katie squeezed back under the wire fence into the garden, Mum was sitting out at the patio table, sketching ideas for new paintings.

"Hello, darling," she said, looking up. Then she added, "Oh my, what's happened to your trousers?"

Katie frowned down at the pink stain soaking its way up her jeans – she must not have rolled them up quite high enough. Seeing the wild strawberry juice made her sad,

because it reminded her of the fun she'd been having with her fairy friends before they got in a mood with her. Of course, Mum would never believe she'd shrunk to fairy size and stood in a bathtub stomping on wild strawberries, so Katie just said, "I think maybe I stepped in some old paint water in my room."

"You're such a mucky pup," said Mum, but as she was an artist and always covered in blobs of paint herself, she didn't *really* mind. "Now, pop upstairs and change your jeans," she called out as Katie wandered inside. "And give that room a tidy-up while you're there! Then after lunch I'll help you put the tent up for tonight."

Katie was still upset about falling out with the fairies, but thinking about the sleepover cheered her up

quite a lot. And, as she and Mum giggled over the wonky tent which they couldn't quite get to stand up, she felt almost back to her usual sunny self.

Lily Rose arrived just as Katie and Mum had hammered in the final tent peg. Then Mum helped them to bake chocolate chip cookies for their midnight feast, and filled a nice big flask with cold milk to go with them. Then she showed Katie how to make a princess hat from cardboard and

old net curtain, and Lily Rose made a tiara from silver foil and glitter.

The afternoon flew by as Katie and Lily Rose collected up dolls, music, games, hairbrushes and bobbles and arranged everything in the tent. Getting ready for the sleepover was so exciting, but now and again Katie felt a pang of sadness

about her argument with the fairies. She really wanted to go down to the almost-meadow and make up with them – but she couldn't with Lily Rose there. And part of her wondered why she

19

should be the first to say sorry – after all, it wasn't *her* who'd been sulky and mean!

When Katie and Lily Rose were sitting at the garden table, drawing out their own board game for the sleepover, Mum came out to get the washing in. She paused by the line, her arms full of clean sheets, looking puzzled.

"I'm sure I put out *four* pillowcases. . ." she began, then she sighed and shook her head. "Oh well, maybe I dropped one on the stairs or left it in the machine."

Katie smiled. Mum was always losing things, so it wasn't at all strange that a pillowcase was missing.

After a lovely tea of homemade tomato soup and cheese sandwiches, Katie and Lily Rose got into their night things, and giggled as they slipped their jackets and shoes back on, because it felt so strange! Katie kissed Mum goodnight and then Lily Rose did too, and they headed out to the tent.

The sleepover was lots of fun, especially when they pretended to be princesses trapped in a castle. Katie wished the fairies were there – they loved made-up games. Even

though she knew it was far too risky for them to come to the sleepover, she did really miss them.

As darkness fell in the garden, Katie and Lily Rose hung the lantern torch from the centre of the tent and played their made-up board game. Katie was just zipping up the tent flap when she saw the light go out in Mum's bedroom window. She and Lily Rose snuggled into their sleeping bags and were soon warm and cosy in the softly glowing lamplight.

For a while they chatted about horse-riding and Ebony, Lily Rose's pony, whom Katie had ridden in the gymkhana. Then Lily Rose said, "I know! Now it's dark, let's tell ghost stories!"

Katie wrinkled up her nose. "I'm not sure," she said. "What if we get spooked out?"

"Oh, we'll be fine," said Lily Rose. "We're only in your garden. There's nothing at all to be afraid of out here, is there?"

Katie had to agree that there wasn't, and soon she was listening wide-eyed to Lily Rose's tale of the headless horseman of old Bridport town. Lily Rose was just telling the part about hearing the pounding of hooves as the ghostly horseman rode by at night, when suddenly a big black shadow flitted past the tent. Katie jumped and grabbed Lily Rose's arm.

"What was that?" she whispered, panicking.

"I'm sure it's nothing," said Lily Rose, and picked up her story.

But then they both saw the shadow flit by again and heard an eerie noise. A *whoooooo* noise. A *ghostly* kind of noise. Katie shuddered and even Lily Rose fell silent, listening intently. Putting a finger to her lips, she crawled over to the zip and very carefully began to undo it, not making a sound. She and Katie grasped each other's hands and, trembling, they both stuck their heads out of the tent.

Then. . .

"Aaaaaaaaaaaaaaahhhhhhhhhh!" they screamed, throwing themselves

back in and zipping the flap up tight.

"A ghost!" cried Lily Rose.

She and Katie huddled together, shaking. Outside there was a proper white ghost with big black empty eyes, hovering and *whooooooo*ing in the air before them.

"Oh, Lily Rose," Katie barely whispered, "what *are* we going to do?"

Chapter 3

When Katie's heart finally stopped hammering, she had a very strange feeling. It was a feeling that something wasn't quite right about the ghost. That maybe the ghost was too, well, sort of *pillowcase*-shaped.

She let go of Lily Rose, crawled over to the tent flap and listened carefully.

The ghost was still going, *"Whoooooo! Whoooooo!"* outside.

"Katie, what *are* you doing?" hissed Lily Rose.

"It's OK. I just want to check something," Katie whispered, and she began to unzip the tent flap.

She stuck her head outside again and there was the ghost, still hovering and *whooooo*ing.

Katie turned back to Lily Rose, who was cowering in her sleeping bag. Giving her a nervous smile, she crawled out, zipped the tent back up behind her and stepped into the darkness.

"WHOOOOOOOOO!" went the ghost, floating in the night air right in front of her.

Katie took a deep breath to steady her nerves and then reached out and grabbed it.

"WHOOOO – eeekkk!!"

That's not a ghostly noise, she thought, holding tight. The little thing squirming in her grip was

definitely not a *ghostly* thing. It was much more like a *fairy* thing. In fact, it was very much like a fairy wearing a pillowcase! She whipped it off, expecting to see naughty Bluebell, then gasped in surprise. Instead there was timid little Snowdrop, holding up two sticks, which she had been using to give the ghost its waving arms.

"Snowdrop!" Katie hissed, letting the little fairy go. "You pinched that pillowcase from the washing line and now it's all muddy and torn, and you've drawn two black eyes on it! What's Mum going to say?"

"I only borrowed it," muttered Snowdrop, hovering in the air. She glanced at the ruined pillowcase regretfully. "And I didn't mean for it to get spoilt."

Katie folded her arms crossly. "And the rest of you had better come out too," she whispered sharply. "I know you're hiding in the shadows!"

Bluebell, Rosehip and Daisy wriggled out from their hiding places among the night-blooming jasmine and flew over.

"Why didn't you stop her? She gave me such a fright!" Katie asked them in a hushed voice.

Rosehip and Daisy hung their heads, and even Bluebell looked a little bit ashamed of herself.

At last, Daisy spoke. "It was Snowdrop's idea and I said she

shouldn't do it but then Bluebell and Rosehip agreed to come with her and I didn't want to stay down in the almost-meadow all on my own," she gabbled, shivering at the thought, "so I had to come too."

"Is this true, Snowdrop?" asked Katie sharply, forgetting to whisper.

"Katie?" called Lily Rose from inside the tent. "Who are you talking to?"

Katie was startled. "No one!" she called. "There's no ghost out here. We must have imagined it. And now I'm just playing let's pretend!"

She grimaced, knowing that Lily Rose would never believe *that* silly excuse in a million years. But perhaps it would keep her from opening the tent flap for a little longer. Long enough for her to ask them a question before sending them

home."But why were you trying to scare us?"

When none of them answered, she said more gently, "Come on, it's OK. You can tell me."

Rosehip glanced at Bluebell and Bluebell nudged Daisy and Daisy gave a little cough and then finally Snowdrop mumbled, "It's just, we were so upset that we couldn't come to the sleepover. We thought that if we scared you you'd go inside and Lily Rose would go home and then there wouldn't *be* a sleepover, so we wouldn't be missing it!"

Katie sighed. "I did *explain* why you couldn't come. I was only trying to protect you," she whispered. "Now really, you must all fly back to the Fairy House before Lily Rose sees you! Go!"

But the fairies didn't move.

Instead they looked longingly towards the softly glowing tent.

"Would it *really* matter if she did see us?" Bluebell began.

"Yes!" cried Katie, exasperated.

"She's so nice. I'm sure she wouldn't tell anyone," said Daisy.

"We could make her promise not to," suggested Rosehip.

"No way," Katie hissed. "Now, go *on*! It's for your own good. . ."

But then a voice behind her cried, "Oh, wow! Are they real?"

Katie whirled round to see Lily Rose's head poking out of the tent, her face a picture of astonishment. She looked from the fairies to Lily Rose and from Lily Rose to the fairies. She didn't know what to do or say. It was too late – Lily Rose had seen them now.

The fairies continued to hover beside

Katie, but not one of them would meet her eye.

"Katie, this is absolutely amazing!" Lily Rose continued, still gaping at them. "*Real* fairies! I just can't believe it!"

Katie sighed deeply and said, "Lily Rose, these are my *very naughty* friends, Bluebell, Rosehip, Daisy and Snowdrop."

The fairies all said *pleased to meet you* in their politest manners and Lily Rose said hello back, between gasps of "Wow!" and "How amazing!"

"You can't tell *anyone*," said Rosehip. "No one's supposed to find out about us. *You* weren't even supposed to."

Lily Rose glanced at Katie, who said, "I can't explain why, but you have to promise to keep the fairies a secret."

"I promise," said Lily Rose solemnly, and Katie and the fairies felt that she really meant it.

Then Bluebell shivered dramatically. "It's getting ever so windy out here," she announced.

"And cold," added Rosehip.

"And I'm *very* scared of the dark," Daisy whimpered.

"Do you think maybe we might be allowed to stay?" asked Snowdrop hopefully.

Lily Rose clapped her hands in delight. "Oh, please let them, Katie," she begged. "Pleeeeeaaaaase!"

Katie rolled her eyes. "Oh, all right," she said at last. Then she turned to her fairy friends and added, "But don't think I'm very

impressed with your behaviour." That was the exact same thing Mum said to *her* sometimes!

The fairies nodded solemnly but they could barely disguise their delight.

Lily Rose squealed. "I can't believe I'm having a sleepover with *real* fairies!"

Katie shooed them into the tent before Mum came to see what all the noise was about.

Once inside, the fairies looked round excitedly, grinning as they took in the storybooks and music player and hairbrushes.

"Come on, you can share our sleeping bags!" cried Lily Rose gleefully.

So Bluebell and Daisy clambered in beside her and Snowdrop and Rosehip climbed in with Katie.

"Sleepy-overs *are* fun!" Bluebell admitted, wriggling about happily.

"I wish we could have special sleepover outfits like yours," said Daisy wistfully to Katie and Lily Rose, gazing at their pink night things in admiration.

"Maybe we can," said Snowdrop shyly.

She glanced up at Katie, who gave her a smile of encouragement.

"Well, it's just you did say that the pillowcase was ruined anyway," she continued, "and I've got my sewing kit and a bottle of wild strawberry juice. . ."

Katie grinned at her. "Go on, then," she said.

Snowdrop rummaged in her secret pocket, and soon the tent was a flurry of activity as Rosehip cut fabric out from the pillowcase to make fairy-

sized pyjamas and Snowdrop sewed along the sides and Daisy dipped them into the wild strawberry juice that Katie had poured into the lid of her flask. The juice soaked into the material in an instant and turned it bright pink ... with magical silver sparkles that winked and twinkled like stars in the night sky.

"Wow!" cried Katie. "I wish *ours* did that!"

Snowdrop smiled. "It's my special ingredient," she told them. "A dash of fairy dust!"

Brave little Bluebell volunteered to hold the sparkling pink pyjamas outside to dry. The wind was so high that she had to hang on tight to the tent flap or she would have been blown away!

Then the fairies decided to decorate the pyjamas with Katie's felt tips. As they were drawing stars and flowers and snowflakes

(you can guess who *that* was!) they all chattered away.

"We were there at the gymkhana where you met Katie," Snowdrop told Lily Rose.

"Were you?" gasped Lily Rose, amazed. "But why didn't I see you?"

"We're good at keeping out of sight!" said Rosehip proudly.

"Not tonight, you weren't!" said

Katie, but she was grinning, and as everyone joined in her laughter, she thought that having the fairies to the sleepover might just work out rather well after all.

"I was the one who taught Katie to ride," Rosehip was telling Lily Rose. "We used some fairy dust to make her toy ponies come alive. It was so much fun!"

Katie smiled at the memory. "I'd never even been on a pony before that," she added.

"Wow," exclaimed Lily Rose. "You mean you'd only just learned to ride and you were jumping and everything? That's really amazing, Katie!" She turned to Rosehip and added, "You must be a brilliant teacher."

Rosehip couldn't help grinning. "Thanks," she said. "And guess

what? Half of my name is the same as half of your name."

"That's true," said Lily Rose. "I hadn't thought of that."

They smiled at each other, and then the other fairies smiled at Lily Rose too.

As the others were chatting, Snowdrop fluttered close to Katie's ear and whispered, "I'm so glad you made friends with Lily Rose, because now she's *our* new friend too."

Katie smiled to herself. "I'm glad you're glad," she whispered back.

Soon the four fairies were wearing their new pyjamas and looking extremely pleased with themselves. Katie put some music on and they paraded up and down the tent, doing twirls and curtsies as if they were in a fashion show.

41

"Now we're really dressed for a sleepy-over!" cried Bluebell, gleefully turning a somersault in the air. "What shall we do next?"

Chapter 4

It was really cosy in the tent with the lantern glowing and the wind blowing up outside. The fairies had voted for hair-styling, so Katie asked for a French plait.

Snowdrop's and Bluebell's wings tickled her neck as they twisted up sections of her long tangly hair, making her giggle. They quickly got confused about which bits of hair were meant to go where and changed their minds so often that

Katie began to feel like a maypole! Lily Rose's hair was shorter, but Rosehip and Daisy didn't  find it any easier to style. In the end the styles they created looked nothing at all like French plaits, but it didn't matter because they were having so much fun.

"Yours looks really strange!" giggled Katie.

"So does yours!" cried Lily Rose.

"Well, I suppose they're not *quite* perfect," Bluebell admitted.

"We'll have to call them something else, something totally original and invented by us," Rosehip said.

"How about Crazy Fairy Braids?" suggested Snowdrop,

making them all giggle.

"Can you do ours now?" asked Bluebell. "We've never had our hair done before. Normally we just sort of let it hang there, but this looks like fun!"

So Katie set out her dolls' brushes and combs, then she and Lily Rose had a wonderful time doing the fairies' hair and putting in bunches and tiny jewelled clips and little braids. When they were finished, she propped up a make-up mirror on a book so that they could see themselves.

"Wow! We look amazing!" cried Bluebell, adjusting the blue stripy band Lily Rose had put in for her.

"We look fantastic," Rosehip agreed, shaking her long flower-filled ponytail in delight.

In fact, the fairies loved their new

looks so much that Katie thought they were never going to stop a d m i r i n g themselves!

"I've got a good idea," said Lily Rose. "Let's tell secrets! That's always fun at a sleepover."

The fairies were so excited about this that they even stopped admiring themselves and snuggled into the sleeping bags instead.

"Right then, Katie, you first," said Lily Rose, grinning. "Tell us a secret."

Katie's eyes twinkled. "I think you've

already found out my secret. My four secrets, that is!" she whispered, and they all laughed.

Then Bluebell put her hand up, which was something she'd learned when she'd turned big and gone to school in Katie's place. "Me next! I'll tell one!"

Katie couldn't help wondering what kinds of secrets fairies had. She and Lily Rose leaned in, intrigued.

"Well, you know the flying egg and spoon race we had at the Fairy School sports day last year?" Bluebell began.

"Yes," said the three other fairies.

Bluebell left a long pause for effect, enjoying being the centre of attention, and then she whispered, "Well, my secret is that Rosehip only won because she stuck her egg

to her spoon with spiders' web!"

Snowdrop and Daisy gasped in shock at this and stared at Rosehip, who went bright red.

"I did not!" she protested. "OK, well, maybe I did a tiny bit, but it still took lots of skill to zigzag in and out of those trees so quickly!"

"You lot haven't got the hang of this at all," said Katie. "You're only supposed to tell your *own* secrets, not other people's!"

But she might as well have been talking to herself, because Rosehip folded her arms and tossed her flame-red hair, eyes glinting in the lamplight.

"Well," she said to Bluebell, "you remember when you made that hat out of dried pondweed and you asked me if I liked it, and I said yes and so you wore it to the Fairy Queen's birthday tea?"

"Yes. So?" said Bluebell.

"Well, I was only saying I liked it to save your feelings, but in actual fact you looked really silly and everyone at the whole party thought you did too, so there," Rosehip finished triumphantly.

Bluebell gasped and clutched her head as if the offending hat were still there. She glared at Rosehip. "How could you do that to me?" she demanded.

But Rosehip just stuck her tongue out at Bluebell, which was the final straw. They both leapt into the air and there was a flurry of wings as they tumbled over and over each other. Daisy and Snowdrop took cover in Katie's sleeping bag, their wings tickling

her legs.
"Let
g o ! "
shouted
Bluebell.
"No, you
let go!"
"No, you!"
"You!"
Lily Rose looked alarmed
but Katie just rolled her eyes. "Don't
worry. They're always like this," she
explained. "They'll stop when. . ."

But she didn't finish what she
was going to say, because there was
a loud noise outside the tent.

A WHOOOOOO!!! noise.

She and Lily Rose sat bolt upright
and stared at each other in shock.

Bluebell and Rosehip stopped
fighting in mid-air and plopped

back on to the sleeping bags.

Snowdrop popped her head out of Katie's sleeping bag and whispered, "What was that?"

"I don't know," Katie whispered back. "But I think *you* do, Snowdrop. Come on, own up. You set something else up outside to scare us, didn't you? And you forgot to take it down."

"It's not me this time," the little fairy croaked. "I promise."

Katie still didn't believe her. But then they heard the *whoooooo!!* noise again, louder this time. Snowdrop squealed and shot so far up into the air that she hit the top of the tent. As she crashed back down on to the

sleeping bag, the lantern lit up her pale face and Katie saw the panic in her eyes. She knew that Snowdrop was telling the truth. She really *hadn't* left anything else outside to scare them.

Then Daisy's head came poking out of the sleeping bag too, her eyes wide with worry. Their quarrel forgotten, Rosehip and Bluebell huddled into Katie's lap with Daisy and Snowdrop.

"WHOOOOOOOOOOOOOOO!!!" went the noise again.

The six friends all froze in fright.

Katie shuddered. "If it's not one

of your tricks, Snowdrop," she hissed, "then what on earth is it?"

Snowdrop's pale face was paler than ever and her slim shoulders shuddered with fear. "I think, maybe, it's a *real* ghost," she whispered.

Chapter 5

"WHOOOOOOOOOOOO!!" went the scary noise again.

"We can't just sit here feeling frightened," said Katie. "We have to find out what's making that noise."

"I'd rather just sit here feeling frightened, thank you very much!" said Daisy, shivering.

"But it might not be a ghost," Katie reasoned. "It might be some kind of animal."

"You mean like a fox?" asked Snowdrop.

"Probably more like a werewolf," muttered Daisy darkly.

"It could be injured," Rosehip said, looking worried.

"It could be *hungry*," Daisy countered.

Katie shrugged, slipped her jacket on over her nightie and pulled her shoes on to her bare feet. She felt relieved when Lily Rose did the same.

Seeing that they were both going outside, the fairies gathered into a little circle in the air and had a quick discussion. When

they broke apart, Bluebell said, "We're coming too."

Katie thanked them all. She crouched at the tent flap, slowly unzipping it, as the fairies hovered nervously beside her. "Come on, then," she whispered, but nobody moved. No one wanted to be first out into the darkness, where the scary noise was.

"Let's go together," suggested Lily Rose.

The fairies all nodded and grasped each other's hands.

Lily Rose grabbed Katie's hand too. "One, two, three, go!" she said, and together they all tumbled out of the tent.

"WHOOOOOOOO!" went the scary noise, making them all jump again.

"It's coming from over there,"

hissed Katie. "From the almost-meadow."

Swinging the lantern before them, the group of friends crept out into the night. The fairies fluttered overhead as Katie and Lily Rose slipped under the wire fence and into the almost-meadow, still tightly clasping one another's hands.

"WHOOOOOOOOOO!" went the scary noise.

Katie gulped and forced her trembling legs to walk towards it.

The strong wind made the friends shiver as they swished through the long grass, following the pool of lamplight across the almost-meadow. Katie's breath was quick with fear – the place she knew so well seemed strange and scary in the dark. They followed the scary noise to an old tree stump. The

lantern lit up the jagged, splintered bark around its hollow and its knarled, knotted roots.

"WHOOOOOOOOOOOOOO!"

This time it was louder than ever.

They squealed in fright – well, all except brave little Bluebell. The scary noise seemed to be coming from *inside* the hollow.

Katie tried to dangle the lantern into the hollow but she was too small to see over the top of it.

"One of us will have to go down there," declared Bluebell, her eyes shining with excitement in the lamplight.

"No one's going

down there," Katie said firmly.

"*I* am," Bluebell insisted. "I'm not scared of some mouldy old ghost! And besides, what if there *is* an injured animal trapped inside?"

"No!" said Katie.

"OK, fine," said Bluebell sulkily.

But then they all got a shock as Rosehip leapt into the hollow and tumble-fluttered down and down and down.

"Rosehip!" they cried.

The other fairies huddled together and peered into the blackness.

Katie groaned. "We shouldn't have mentioned injured animals – we might have known she'd go rushing down there."

There was silence.

"Rosehip?" called Lily Rose.

Then, "Yikes! Yeek! Help!" screeched Rosehip, from far below. "Something's got me! It's a ghost, a *ghoooooost*! It's tangling me up! Heeeeeelp!"

The fairies looked at Katie in panic. Katie looked at Lily Rose. No one knew what to do.

"WHOOOOOOOOO!!!" went the spooky noise, rushing around them again.

They all jumped in fright . . . except for Katie. She stood still, listening intently. Then she cried, "Aha!"

Rosehip was still screeching and thrashing about down below, but Katie called out, "Calm down, there's no ghost! The spooky noise is nothing but the wind whooshing

60

over the top of the hollow. It's acting like a whistle! Listen."

The wind blew up again and the spooky noise went "WHOOOOOO!!!" They listened hard and this time they could tell that it wasn't ghostly at all, but just the wind, as Katie had said.

"Phew!" called Rosehip. "But even if it's not a ghost, I'm tangled up in *something*. It's all round my wings, and my arms and legs are stuck too, and I can't flutter back up and, oh, it's very dark down here and. . ." There was a pause and then, in a small trembly voice that didn't sound like Rosehip's at all, she added, "Katie, I'm a little bit scared. What if I'm stuck down here for ever and I can't get out?"

"Don't worry," called Katie. "We'll save you." But she had no idea how.

First, Lily Rose tried lifting Katie up, but even then she couldn't stretch far enough into the hollow to reach Rosehip. She found a twig on the ground and tried sticking that down too. It was long enough, but Rosehip couldn't grab hold of it, because her arms were so tied up in the tangly thing.

"Maybe I could just pop down there and—" Bluebell began hopefully, but Katie said, "No way. No one else is going down there! We don't know what the tangly thing *is*, and Rosehip's already stuck. We can't lose anyone else!" And even Bluebell had to agree that she was right.

They all thought for a long time, but no one had any good ideas. Rosehip tried singing a fairy song to keep her spirits up, but her voice

was small and shaky, and she soon trailed off into silence.

After a long while, shy little Snowdrop said, "I've got an idea. I think I know how we can rescue Rosehip without getting tangled up ourselves."

They all leaned in to listen. "Yes?" said Katie encouragingly.

"Well, if we don't touch the bottom of the hollow, we can't get tangled up, can we?" she reasoned. "So, we have to *dangle*. We can make a fairy chain and you can lower us down the hollow and the fairy on the end of the chain can pull Rosehip up."

They all agreed that Snowdrop's idea was good thinking. The only problem was that Daisy was too scared of the dark to go dangling down inside a hollow tree. Luckily Snowdrop came up with another

good idea. She picked three daisies and pulled a little bottle of fairy dust from her secret pocket. She dabbed a tiny bit into the centre of each daisy and soon they glowed like torches. Daisy, Rosehip and Snowdrop each put one on their heads and helped each other to tie the stalks up tight.

"Brilliant thinking, Snowdrop,"

cried Bluebell, sweeping her torch beam from left to right just by moving her neck. "Now we can see what we're doing down there!"

Snowdrop smiled shyly. "I just hope my plan works," she said.

Their hearts were all pounding hard. Katie wished everyone luck, then they put the plan into action. Katie held on to Daisy's feet and Daisy held on to Bluebell's feet and Bluebell held on to Snowdrop's feet and Snowdrop dangled in the air, arms flailing. Lily Rose lifted Katie up as high as she could and Katie leaned over the hollow and carefully lowered the fairy chain down and

down and down.

Eventually, Snowdrop's daisy torch cast its light on a cold and dirty, but very relieved, Rosehip. Snowdrop stretched out for her, but she couldn't quite reach. "Katie, can you just lean over a bit further," she called.

Katie did, but this made the fairy chain swing from side to side.

"Urgh! I think I'm going to be sick!" groaned Daisy.

"You'd better not be!" squealed Bluebell.

Snowdrop stretched as far as she could and her fingers brushed Rosehip's wing. "I just need to get down a tiny bit more," she called.

Katie's arm hurt horribly, but with one final heave she stretched an inch more. "OK, try now," she gasped, winded with the effort.

Snowdrop gritted her teeth and reached just that little bit further until – "Got you!" she cried, grabbing hold of Rosehip's elbow.

"Yay!" the fairies cheered.

Katie grinned. "Hold tight, everyone. We're going up!"

Carefully she lifted Daisy's feet, and three fairies and the tangled-up Rosehip all came out of the hollow.

Katie held Rosehip up to the lamplight and frowned. The little fairy was tied up in some kind of silvery chain. Katie tugged at part of it, but Rosehip just squealed, "Yee-ouch!"

"It's going to take a while to untangle you," Katie explained. "We'd better go back to the tent and do it there."

Soon they were all cosy and warm again in the tent, looking amazed to find that Rosehip was in fact tangled up in a *necklace*! Katie

carefully pulled at one bit and then another, until finally Rosehip was free. She whooped with joy, waving her arms and legs, then zoomed over to the other fairies and hugged them tight, singing, "Thank you for rescuing me!" over and over again.

"It was Snowdrop's idea," said Daisy.

Snowdrop blushed. "It was all of us," she insisted.

"Three cheers for Snowdrop," shouted Bluebell. "Hip, hip. . ."

"Hooray!" cried the other fairies and Katie and Lily Rose.

After one cheer, Snowdrop smiled. After two cheers, she grinned widely. And after three cheers, she was beaming and positively glowing with happiness!

When they'd finished cheering for

Snowdrop, Katie held up the necklace. On the fine chain swung an oval-shaped piece of silver with a gemstone set into it. The gemstone was an amazing pearly blue-green colour and when it caught the lamplight it had the most incredible rainbow sheen to it.

"It's so beautiful," Snowdrop gasped.

"How old do you think it is?" asked Lily Rose.

"And who did it belong to?" wondered Rosehip.

"And what was it doing in that hollow tree?" Daisy added.

As the pendant swung and twisted on its chain, Katie noticed something. She held it right up to her eyes and squinted at it. Then she ran her fingers along the edge of the silver. Yes, she was right – it had

tiny *hinges*. "This isn't just a necklace!" she whispered. "It's a *locket*! If I just. . ." She fiddled with the catches and suddenly the front of the necklace opened up.

The fairies all gasped and squealed with excitement.

Inside the locket was a teeny tiny piece of paper. Katie handed it to Snowdrop, who unfolded it very, very carefully, to make sure it didn't tear.

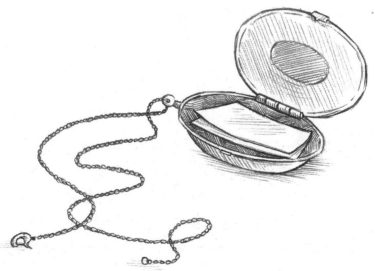

The shyest little fairy studied it carefully. "There's writing on it," she murmured, eyes wide in wonderment.

Indeed, the piece of paper was a teeny tiny letter written in teeny tiny writing.

To The Finder of This Letter

My name is Elizabeth May and I am eighteen years old. I have lived all my life in a cottage beside these fields. I'm sure that once I saw a fairy here, out of the corner of my eye. Now I'm off to be a governess and I wish to leave something of mine in this, my favourite place. I hope you will treasure it, and this meadow, as much as I have done, and make good use of them both.

Elizabeth

They all gazed at the letter, astonished.

"I bet Elizabeth really did see a fairy!" said Bluebell excitedly.

"Maybe it was our friend Foxglove. I think she was once given a fairy task near here," cried Daisy.

"This must all have been fields once, before it was built on, wasn't it, Katie?" said Lily Rose.

But Katie was lost in thought and didn't reply.

They all turned to find her staring from the letter to the necklace and back again, a smile spreading slowly across her face.

"Katie?" said Lily Rose again.

Katie started. "You do realize what this is, don't you?" she asked them all.

"Of course. A silver locket with a

pretty stone in," Daisy replied.

"What about it?" asked Bluebell impatiently.

"The stone is an *opal*," said Katie. "And what is opal?"

She couldn't help grinning as the fairies all ummed and ahhed, still not sure what she was talking about.

Then suddenly Snowdrop cried, "It's one of the twelve birthstones! The Fairy Queen must have been secretly guiding us to find it! Opal is one of the special gems that we need to. . ."

But Katie quickly put a finger to her lips. While Lily Rose knew about the fairies, she still didn't want her to find out everything about the birthstones and the fairy task as well. Snowdrop suddenly understood and clamped her lips tight shut.

"Well, Elizabeth hoped the finder would put the opal necklace to good

use and we will, won't we?" Katie asked the fairies, with a secret wink.

"Yes, we certainly will," they all agreed, laughing.

Lily Rose gave them a puzzled look and then joined in the laughter too, although of course she didn't know why they were quite so happy about finding an old locket.

"Oh, look, it's almost twelve o'clock," said Lily Rose, holding her watch up to the lamp for them to see.

"Time for our midnight feast!" cried Katie excitedly. She pulled the tub of chocolate chip cookies from her bag and Lily Rose opened the flask of milk to go with them.

Snowdrop flew over and peered into the flask. "I know what would make that drink extra-specially yummy," she said.

With a twinkle in her eye, she

pulled her silky petal skirt towards her and rummaged in the secret pocket. She pulled out a bottle of pink juice and tipped some into the flask. When Katie poured out the milk – into cups for her and Lily Rose, and acorn cups for the fairies – it had turned pink!

"It's wild strawberry sparkle-shake surprise!" Snowdrop announced proudly. "My very own recipe!"

Katie took a big gulp and squealed in amazement when a stream of pink bubbles came out of her mouth and popped in a shower of sparkles on the top of the tent. They all giggled and Snowdrop said, *"That's* the surprise!"

Soon they were

happily munching on chocolate chip cookies and blowing wild strawberry sparkle-shake bubbles and retelling their spooky adventure over and over again. By the third telling, they were certain that Rosehip had *definitely* been stuck for *ever and ever* and that it had been the *greatest ever* rescue in the whole history of fairy rescues.

When all the cookies were gone and the last wild strawberry sparkle-shake bubble had popped, they all snuggled down inside their sleeping bags, desperately pretending not to be tired.

"This sleepy-over is *so* much fun!" Bluebell exclaimed. "What shall we do next?"

"I know, let's stay awake all night and invent fairy stories!" giggled Rosehip. "I'll start. Once upon a time. . ."

But she didn't get any further than that, because, like the other little fairies and Katie and Lily Rose, she had fallen fast asleep.

The next morning Katie and Lily Rose sat at the garden table, munching toast, as the fairies played among the breakfast things. In the hazy morning sunshine, the garden and the almost-meadow looked bright and friendly and Katie could hardly believe that they'd been so frightened just a few hours ago. And of nothing but the wind!

When Mum came out with some more toast, the fairies ducked behind a cereal box, just in case she had suddenly started to be able to see them.

"Thank you so much for having

me for the sleepover," said Lily Rose, grinning up at her. "It really *was* magical!" she added, with a quick wink at Katie.

Mum smiled. "You're welcome. Come back again any time, won't you?" she said, and wandered back towards the kitchen.

When Mum was safely inside, the fairies came out from behind the cereal box. Soon Rosehip and Bluebell were playing see-saw on a

fork laid over an upturned marmalade jar, and Snowdrop was making a snowman out of butter.

Daisy was leaning as far as she could into the jam pot, licking her lips and trying to dip her finger in. She leaned further and further until –
"Whaaaaaa!" she cried, tumbling in.

When Katie had fished her out with a teaspoon and deposited her safely on top of the table, Daisy said

to Rosehip, "Phew! That was scary! Now I know how you felt when you got stuck in that hollow!"

"Daisy, it's hardly the same," scoffed Bluebell, but Rosehip was rather sweet and agreed that it was *exactly* the same and that Daisy was very brave too.

Daisy grinned as she scooped a

blob of jam from her cheek and tasted it. "Yum! Almost as good as our wild strawberry sparkle-shake surprise!" she exclaimed.

"Oh, no! I've just realized something," said Katie. "That drink had had Bluebell's smelly feet in it!"

"Really? Urgh!" squealed Lily Rose.

"For the last time, my feet are NOT smelly!" shouted Bluebell, which set the other fairies off giggling again.

"Oh, you know we don't mean it!" cried Snowdrop. "We love you really!"

And with that they all wrapped her into a big fairy hug.

Katie couldn't help grinning. She felt like the luckiest girl in the world to have four little friends like Daisy, Bluebell, Rosehip and Snowdrop.

And besides, the sun was shining, they had another one of the birthstones, and she was certain that the new day would bring them a whole new adventure!

The End

Bluebell
Spring fairy

Likes:

blue, blue, blue and more blue,
turning somersaults in the air, dancing

Dislikes:

coming second, being told what to do

Daisy
Summer fairy

Likes:

everyone to be friends, bright sunshine,
cheery yellow colours, smiling

Dislikes:

arguments, cold dark places,
orange nylon dresses

Rosehip
Autumn fairy

Likes:

riding magic ponies, telling Bluebell
what to do, playing the piano, singing

Dislikes:

keeping quiet, boring colours,
not being the centre of attention!

Snowdrop
Winter fairy

Likes:

singing fairy songs, cool quiet places, riding her
favourite magical unicorn, making snowfairies

Dislikes:

being too hot, keeping secrets

Don't miss the rest of the series!

Kelly McKain

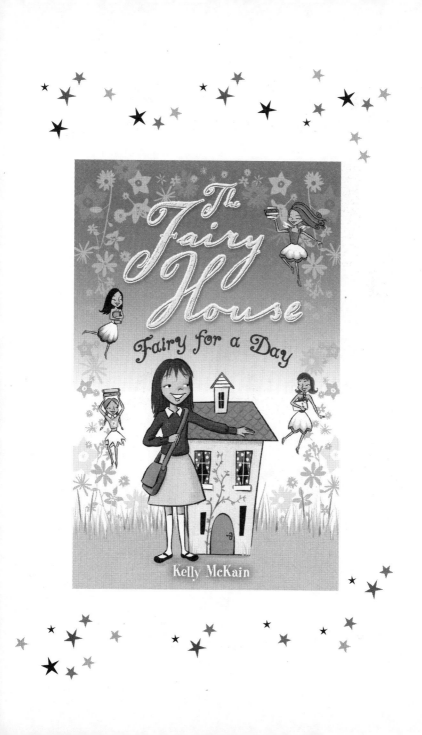

The Fairy House

Fairy for a Day

Kelly McKain

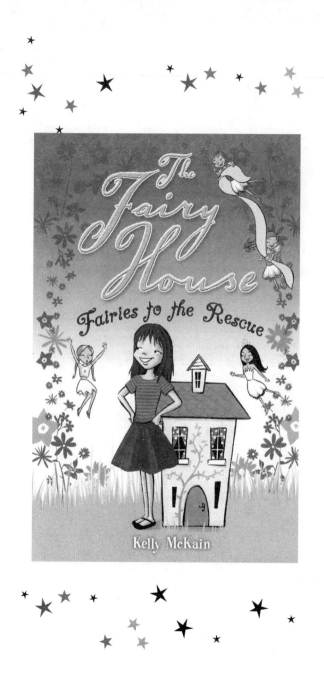

The Fairy House

Fairies to the Rescue

Kelly McKain

The Fairy House

Fairy Riding School

Kelly McKain

The Fairy House

Fairy Jewels

Kelly McKain